Feathers and Fools

MEM FOX

Feathers and Fools

Illustrated by Nicholas Wilton

HARCOURT BRACE & COMPANY

San Diego   New York   London

Requests for permission to make copies
of any part of the work should be mailed to:
Permissions Department, Harcourt Brace & Company,
6277 Sea Harbor Drive, Orlando, Florida 32887-6777.

Library of Congress Cataloging-in-Publication Data
Fox, Mem 1946—
Feathers and fools/Mem Fox: illustrated by Nicholas Wilton.
p.   cm.
Summary: A modern fable about some peacocks and swans
who allow the fear of their differences to become so great
that they end up destroying each other.
ISBN 0-15-200473-4
[1. Fables. 2. Peacocks—Fiction. 3. Swans—Fiction.]
I. Wilton, Nicholas, ill.   II. Title.
PZ8.2.F65Fe   1996
[E]—dc20   95-10707

First edition
A B C D E

Printed in Singapore

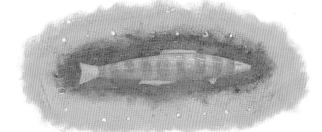

In a rambling garden, long ago and far away, there lived a pride of magnificent peacocks.

Nearby, in the rushes and reeds of a clear blue lake, dwelt a flock of elegant swans.

One day, a peacock, musing on the mysteries of life, said, "How strange that swans should swim. It is fortunate indeed that we do not, for we should surely drown."

The other peacocks pecked and strutted, contemplating the meaning of this profound observation.

Again the first peacock spoke. "How strange that swans should fly. It is happy indeed that we do not, for we should surely look ridiculous."

The other peacocks pecked and strutted again, contemplating the meaning of this second observation.

Again the first peacock broke the silence. "I fear the swans," he said. "They have great strength. If they wished, they could turn us out of our gardens, or make us fly, or force us to swim."

Here and there, peacock feathers rustled uneasily. "Alas!" cried one. "No home! No happiness! No life!" There followed anxious mutterings and a making of plans.

And so it came to pass that the peacocks gathered a great quantity of feathers which they sharpened into arrows and concealed in the shadows of their gardens.

"Now we can defend ourselves against the swans," said the first-and-most-foolish peacock, raising his voice that the swans might hear. "We shall hurl these arrows at their throats and slaughter every one should they ever try to change our way of life."

The swans, in fear, heard these fighting words and sharpened feathers of their own in even greater numbers and concealed them cleverly among the rushes and reeds.

Both sides, for safety's sake, continued to add to their weapons, but in dismay each discovered that the more arrows they acquired, the more terrified they became.

At night, in the gardens and on the lake, no birds slept. Every sound made their hearts race. Every movement made them tremble.

One day a swan flew high over the peacocks, bearing in her beak a reed for nest-making.

The peacocks in a panic mistook it for an arrow and gathering their forces bore swiftly down upon the lake.

But the swans, seeing them coming, made ready.
Soon cries filled the air and blood darkened the earth.
A cloud of feathers rose into the sky and haunted the sun.

Of all the birds, not one remained alive.
Silence hung over the gardens.
And over the lake.

Then, in the shadows of the gardens, an egg hatched, and
a small bird staggered out into the bloodstained stillness.

Among the reeds beside the lake a second egg hatched, and another small bird teetered out into the ruins.

They stumbled towards each other, alive with curiosity and trust.

"You're just like me," said the first. "You have feathers and two legs."

"You're just like me," said the second. "You have a head and two eyes."

"Shall we be friends?" asked the first.
"Most certainly," replied the second.
So off they went together, in peace and
unafraid, to face the day and share the world.

The illustrations in this book were done in acrylic on illustration board.

The display type was set in Mona Lisa Recut.

The text type was set in Cochin.

Color separations by Bright Arts, Ltd., Singapore

Printed and bound by Tien Wah Press, Singapore

This book was printed with soya-based inks on Leykam recycled paper, which contains more than 20 percent postconsumer waste and has a total recycled content of at least 50 percent.

Production supervision by Warren Wallerstein and Ginger Boyer

Designed by Linda Lockowitz